Cara's Kindness

KRISTI YAMAGUCHI

ILLUSTRATED BY JOHN LEE

sourcebooks
jabberwocky

John Lee created the art using Adobe Photoshop CC.

Published by Sourcebooks Jabberwocky, an imprint of Sourcebooks, Inc.
P.O. Box 4410, Naperville, Illinois 60567-4410
(630) 961-3900
Fax: (630) 961-2168
www.sourcebooks.com

Library of Congress Cataloging-in-Publication data is on file with the publisher.

Source of Production: Phoenix Color, Hagerstown, Maryland, USA
Date of Production: August 2016
Run Number: 5007317

Printed and bound in the United States of America.
PHC 10 9 8 7 6 5 4 3 2 1

To Keara and Emma.
May kindness always be with you,
whether giving or receiving throughout this adventure we call life.
Love you until the last number,
Mom
K. Y.

For Nathan and Samantha.
J. L.

C ara the Cat was practicing at the Ice House skating rink. She was listening to different pieces of music for her upcoming performance, but nothing sounded right.

Then, she noticed one little guy off to the side, watching with a sad face.

She skated over to him. "Hi, I'm Cara. As in caring about why you look so down."

"Hi, I'm Darby the Dog," he responded. "And, well...I don't know how to skate, and I'm...a little afraid to try."

"Aha!" exclaimed Cara. "I can give you a helping hand with that. Let's go!"

Cara guided Darby onto the ice. "Whoa! I'm for sure going to fall down," said a worried Darby.

"Well, of course! That's part of skating," said Cara. "So the first thing you need to learn is how to get back up."

Darby fell down a few times. But Cara helped him up...

and pretty soon, he was skating!

"You rock, Cara!" said Darby. "Now I can go join my friends. Thanks so much!"

"No worries...just pass on the kindness!" replied Cara with a smile.

Darby was hungry from skating and playing tag. As he sat down to have a PB&J and a juice box, he heard a rumbling sound that grew so loud he jumped! Darby looked around.

"Ahhhhh." Pax the Polar Bear looked over to him. "I forgot my lunchbox," he grumbled.

"Well, guess what?" replied Darby. "I have enough for two."

They shared some nibbles and sips and treats. "Mmmmm, that was yummy for my tummy," said a happy Pax. "You're the best, Darby. Thanks so much!"

"No worries...just pass on the kindness!" replied Darby with a smile.

As they were heading home from the rink, Pax asked Cara,
"Have you found the right music yet?"

"No," sighed Cara. "I know the right piece is out there.
I just haven't heard it yet."

Suddenly, they saw Marky the Monkey.

"What are you doing?" asked Cara. "Practicing falling out of a tree?"

"Nope, my ball bounced into the lake, and there's no way I am going into that freezing water!" responded Marky.

"Stand back if you don't want to get wet!" roared Pax as he flew through the air and landed with a giant splash.

He gracefully glided through the water, fetched Marky's ball, and tossed it back to him.

"Sweet!" exclaimed Marky. "Thank you so much, Pax!"

"No worries...just pass on the kindness!" replied Pax with a smile.

The next day, as they were playing kickball, Cara noticed the new girl in school watching them. She was peeking from behind a tree.

"Hey, Marky, let's go over and say hi," said Cara.

They walked up to her.

"Hello, I'm Cara. And this is my friend Marky."

"I'm Samantha the Skunk," she said shyly.

"How do you like the school so far?" asked Marky.

"It's fine. But I do miss playing kickball," she said.

"Well, come pitch for us!" Marky said.

Samantha rolled the ball to Marky, who kicked it high up in the air toward Cara. She caught it and tossed the ball back to Samantha.

"That was great. Thanks for letting me join the team!" Samantha exclaimed.

"No worries...just pass on the kindness!" replied Marky with a smile.

A week later, Cara, Samantha, and Pax were cheering on Darby at their school's championship hockey game.

"This is so exciting!" chimed Cara. "We haven't won the state championship in sixteen years!"

Milo the Mole sat down next to Cara. "Hey, Cara, any luck with your music?" he asked.

Cara sighed. "Still listening, but I haven't heard the right song yet."

Cara introduced Samantha to Milo. "How do you do?" said Milo. "I'm glad you've met our caring friend Cara. I'm blind, so she usually tells me who scores so I know what all the cheering is about."

"I love hockey and I can give you a play-by-play of the game!" Samantha said excitedly.

"He takes the puck away, passes it up to the forward...

who goes around the net...

He shoots... He SCORES!"

Milo jumped up and cheered. He felt like he was really part of the game today.

"Thank you, Samantha!" Milo said as he hugged her.

"No worries...just pass on the kindness," replied Samantha with a smile.

The next week at school, the students were still celebrating. But Cara was worried because today was her showcase performance and all her friends had come to support her.

"Ooooh, I'm feeling butterflies in my stomach," said Cara. "The music is still not right for me... I need help."

"Maybe my good luck present will help with your butterflies," replied Milo. "I'd like to play a special song I wrote for your performance."

"Wow," gasped Cara. "Thank you. It means so much to have the support of friends like you."

As Milo played the piano, the joyful melody inspired Cara. She wowed the audience with her jumps and spins and footwork. And at the end, everyone gave her a standing ovation!

Cara was so happy! She knew
that caring and passing on a small
kindness, one good deed at a time,
had come full circle right back to her.

Caring makes a big difference.